Cheyenne Again

by Eve Bunting ◆ illustrated by Irving Toddy

Clarion Books ◆ New York

My thanks to Peter J. Blodgett, Curator of Western Historical Manuscripts,
the Huntington Library, California; and Eli Paul, Senior Research Historian,
Nebraska State Historical Society.
—E.B.

Clarion Books
a Houghton Mifflin Company imprint
215 Park Avenue South, New York, NY 10003
Text copyright © 1995 by Eve Bunting
Illustrations copyright © 1995 by Irving Toddy

The illustrations for this book were executed in acrylic and oil paint on watercolor paper.
The text is set in 16/20-point Amasis.

For information about permission to reproduce selections from this book
write to Permissions, Houghton Mifflin Company,
215 Park Avenue South, New York, NY 10003.

Printed in the USA

Library of Congress Cataloging-in-Publication Data

Bunting, Eve, 1928–
Cheyenne again / by Eve Bunting ; illustrated by Irving Toddy.
p.   cm.
Summary: In the late 1880's, a Cheyenne boy named Young
Bull is taken to a boarding school to learn the white man's ways.
ISBN 0-396-70364-6
[1. Cheyenne Indians—Ethnic identity—Fiction.
2. Boarding school—Fiction.]   I. Toddy, Irving, ill.   II. Title.
PZ7.B9152Chf   1995   94-43287
CIP
AC

HOR   10   9   8   7   6   5   4   3   2   1

For Christine Bunting, University of California,
Santa Cruz
—E.B.

To all the students of Intermountain Indian School,
Brigham City, Utah
—I.T.

One day he comes,
The Man Who Counts,
and says:
"A boy, aged ten.
He has to go!"
And when he comes again
he has with him
the tall policeman
in his White Man's clothes,
the one called Taking Man.
He wears the hat and spurs,
the gleaming silver badge,
that mark his work.

"Run! Run! Run fast," my mother tells me.
"Hide!"
But, "No!" my father says.
"Young Bull must leave.
Now is the White Man's world.
He needs to learn the White Man's ways.
The corn is drying out.
There will be food
in this place they call school.
Young Bull must go."

And so they walk me to the train,
The Man Who Counts and Taking Man.
"You will speak English,"
says Taking Man.
"It will be better so."
He shines his shining badge.
I do not want to be like him.

"This is the Sleeping Room," they tell me at the school.
So bare a place.
The beds in rows.
No huddle of my brothers, warm around.
No smell of smoke.
No robe spread on the ground.

I will be lonely here.

They take away my buckskins
and my shirt.
The deerskin moccasins my mother made.
They cut my braids,
give me a uniform
of scratchy wool
the color of an ashen sky,
with buttons to the neck.
"No more Cheyenne," they say.
"You have lost
nothing of value.
You will be like us."

I learn geography, arithmetic,
and writing
in the English tongue.
The history of their United States.
I look, but in the book
I cannot see
the Victory of Greasy Grass
where General Custer and his men
attacked our brave Cheyenne and Sioux.
It does not tell
how we defeated them
and counted coup
and left the dead
asleep beside the river there.
My people speak of this with so much pride.
The book leaves it unsaid.

"Attend your lessons,
do not sit and dream," the teacher says.
"You want to be dumb Indian all your life?"
I toss my head.

The bugle calls us in to dinner
and to work.
There's carpentry,
so we who lived in teepees
can repair
the wooden buildings where we sleep
and shed our tears.
We drill like soldiers
and we march, to keep us out of mischief,
so they say.

We march in boots that hurt our feet
so used to softness.
Go to church.
Learn of the White Man's God
and of his love.
We never speak Cheyenne
or talk of the Great Spirit,
the One who raised us in this land.
The Indian in us must disappear, they say.
It must be tamed.

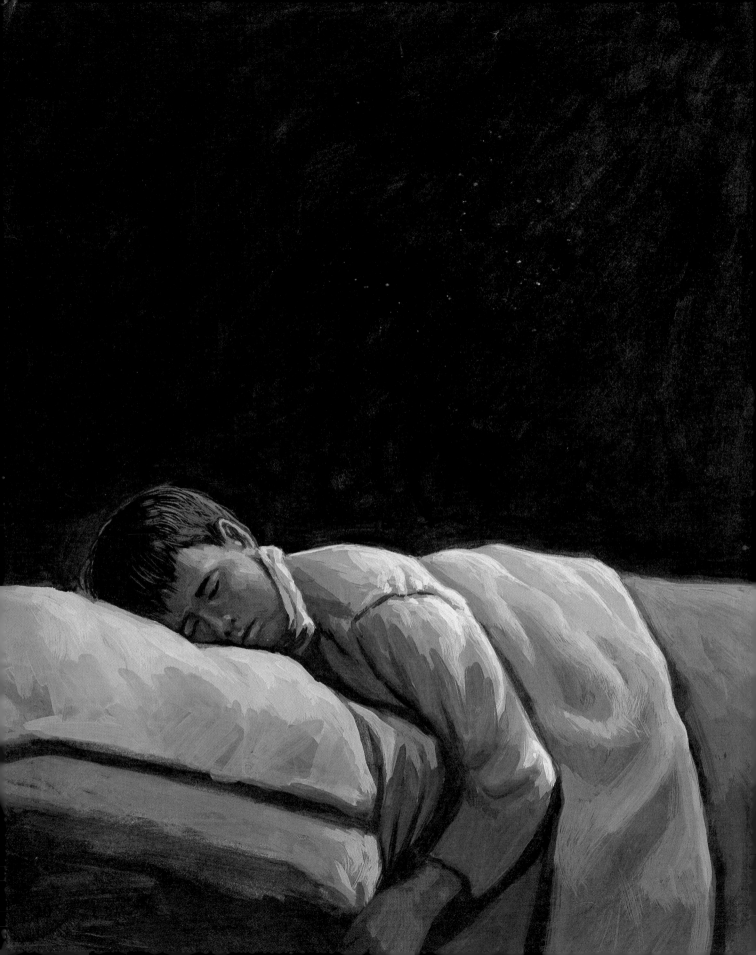

At night I hear the train.
I hear the rain
and cry for home.

One time, the time of the cold moon,
I run away.

The snow is deep.
I have no horse,
no food to take with me.
I only have the stone
my mother gave me once,
a stone that wears the scar of wind and rain
and still is strong.
I hold it fast
to give me strength.

A blizzard roars across the plains
and catches me
so I can run no more.

The trackers find me there
and bring me back.
The school will pay
five dollars cash
for any runaway.

They lock a ball and chain
around my ankle
for one day.
"We must have discipline," they say.

There is one teacher here I like.
"Our world is changing fast," she says.
"We all must change.
I think you will be glad someday
of what you've learned,
though it was hard."
She gives me salve
to soothe the place the chain has rubbed.
"Never forget
that you are Indian inside.
Don't let us take your memories."

I draw
on paper that is lined,
torn from my ledger book.
Across the page
two warriors ride
on painted ponies.
One wears a bonnet with full tail.
His yellow leggings have a bright green fringe.
His breechclout's red.
The other has a shield with yellow bands.
I saw them once like this
against a Cheyenne sky.

The lines across the page
are thin and straight as fencing.

I snip the wire and thrust through.

And in my mind
the warriors and I
ride side by side across the golden plain.

Cheyenne again.

Afterword

In the late 1880s there were twenty-five off-reservation Indian boarding schools across the United States. Indian children were often forced to attend these schools, even against the wishes of their parents.

The first school to be established was Carlisle in Pennsylvania under the leadership of Captain Richard Henry Pratt. Its motto was "From Savagery Into Civilization," and its goal was to separate Indian children from their backgrounds and culture.

Among other such boarding schools were Chemawa in Oregon, Chilocco in Oklahoma, Genoa in Nebraska, Haskell in Kansas. They had the same goals.

Boarding schools for Native American children still exist. But they are now more sensitive to the young people's needs and encourage them to treasure their skills and take pride in their heritage.